S0-DTB-361

Sebastian's Collection Connection

By Gwen Molnar

Illustrated by Mia Hansen

A Hodgepog Book

Copyright © Gwen Molnar
Cover and Inside Illustrations © Mia Hansen

All rights reserved. No part of this book may be reproduced or transmitted in any form or by any means, electronic or mechanical, including photocopying, recording, or by any information storage and retrieval system, without permission in writing from the author and the publisher, except by a reviewer or an academic who may quote brief passages in a review or critical study

All characters in this story are fictitious.

Hodgepog Books gratefully acknowledges the ongoing support of the Canada Council for the Arts

Editors for Press:
Luanne Armstrong, Dorothy Woodend, Amanda Gibbs

Cover design by Dorothy Woodend
Inside layout by Dorothy Woodend
Set in Giddyup and Helvetica in Quark XPress 4.1
Printed at Hignell Press

A Hodgepog Book for Kids
Published in Canada by Hodgepog Books
3476 Tupper Street
Vancouver, British Columbia V5Z 3B7
Phone: (604) 879-3079 Fax: (604) 681-1431
Email: dorothy@axion.net

Canadian Cataloguing in Publishing Data
Molnar Gwen.
    Sebastian's Collection Connection

ISBN 0-9686899-6-5

    1. Collectors and collecting—Juvenile fiction.
    I. Mia Hansen   II. Title

PS8576.O4515S42 2001   jC813'.54   C2001-911189-4
PZ7.M735Se 2001

The Canada Council | Le Conseil des Arts
for the Arts | du Canada

**For old friends
Gunda McConnell
and Dora Armstrong**

Table of Contents

Chapter One
Sebastian's Midnight Visit

Knock. Knock. Knock. Sebastian knocked softly on the door of his father's office. Sebastian was in his pyjamas . He was supposed to be asleep.

"It's me, Sebastian," said Sebastian in a low voice.

"Come on in, Sebastian," said his father. Sebastian turned the door handle and opened the door.

"Hello, Dad," said Sebastian.

"Hello, Sebastian," said Dad. "You're up mighty

late. It's almost midnight."

"I know," said Sebastian. He looked around the tiny room. There was just room for a desk and chair, a filing cabinet and a bookcase. A small computer and a printer sat on the desk. All around the computer were piles of papers.

"I'm glad you came to visit me, Sebastian," said Dad. "I needed a break." He pushed his glasses up and rubbed his eyes.

"Dad?" said Sebastian.

"Yes, Sebastian," said Dad.

"Did you know Margaret has brought all her Barbie dolls with her? She has nine Barbies and she says it's a real collection." Margaret was Sebastian's cousin. Margaret was staying at Sebastian's house for spring break. Sebastian's little sister Jennifer was staying at Margaret's house. Sebastian liked Margaret but she was sometimes very bossy.

"It sounds like a real collection to me," said Dad.

"Well, Dad," said Sebastian. "I want a real collection of SOMETHING too. And I want it by tomorrow morning when Margaret wakes up."

"Hum," said Dad. He always said 'hum' whenever he wanted to think. "Let's think what your collection could be."

"I've thought and thought," said Sebastian. "I

couldn't get to sleep because I was thinking so hard. I have two bears and two dogs and two of a lot of other things. But I really don't want to collect any more of any of those things."

"Hum," said Dad again. "All I collect is money so I can pay all our bills."

Sebastian thought about his money. All his pennies were in one of his banks. All his nickels and dimes and quarters were in another.

"I have two banks," said Sebastian. "I would like to collect more of them."

"I have a little old silver dime bank somewhere in the basement," said Dad. "Banks are a great idea for a collection. "I'll find the dime bank when I get back on the weekend."

"And could you buy me another one when you're gone?"

"I'll try," said Dad.

"Great!' said Sebastian. He gave his dad a hug. "I knew you'd help me."

Back in his room, Sebastian put his two banks on his table. He thought about the little old silver dime bank his dad would find for him on Friday. He thought about the new bank his dad would bring him from his trip. And he thought about another very special bank that he was sure would soon be his.

"I'll be able to sleep now," said Sebastian. He

made up a rhyme about his new collection.

Banks are a wonderful thing to collect
I have two and soon I will have four,
Then five, six and seven,
Eight, nine, ten, eleven,
And goodness knows how many more!

Chapter Two
Two Isn't Enough

"Two of anything doesn't mean it's a collection," said Margaret. Margaret and Sebastian were looking at the little table under Sebastian's bedroom window.

Sebastian's two banks were on the table. One bank was red. It looked like a mail box. Sebastian's Aunt Katie had sent it for his seventh birthday last week. The other bank was gold. It looked like a pirate's chest. It was very old.

"I said it was the start of a collection," said Sebastian. "By Friday, I could have three more banks."

"Where will you get three more banks by Friday?" asked Margaret.

"Well," said Sebastian. "Dad has a little old silver dime bank somewhere. He will find it for me when he gets home from his selling trip on Friday."

Sebastian's dad sold candy to little stores in little towns all over Alberta. When he got home on Fridays, he was very, very tired.

Sebastian's dad was Margaret's favourite uncle. She called him "Uncle Johnnie".

"If Uncle Johnnie gives you his little old silver

dime bank, you will have three banks," said Margaret. "Where will you get two more banks by Friday?"

Sebastian smiled, "Dad's bringing me a new one on Friday."

"That makes four," said Margaret. "How about bank number five?"

Chapter Three
Grandma Emily says, "NO"

"Do you want to come shopping with Margaret and me?" asked Sebastian's mother.

"No, thank you," said Sebastian. "I do not want to go shopping. I want to visit Grandma Emily and Mr. Grandpa. Will you take me over to their house?"

Sebastian was lucky. He had two grandmothers and one grandfather all living in Edmonton.

"I'll call and see if they are home," said Sebastian's mother.

"Grandma Emily is at home, Sebastian," said his mother. "She would love to have you come and visit."

"Good," said Sebastian. "But where is Mr. Grandpa?"

"He has gone to visit a sick friend," said Sebastian's mother.

Sebastian waved goodbye to his mother and Margaret as Grandma Emily opened her front door.

"I'm so glad you came for a visit, Sebastian," said Grandma Emily.

"I'm glad you were home," said Sebastian. "I did not want to go shopping with Mother and Margaret. They always want to look at dumb things like girls' clothes."

Sebastian looked around Grandma Emily's kitchen. On a high shelf in the corner stood Grandma Emily's big glass piggy bank.

"Did you know I'm collecting banks?" asked Sebastian.

"Well, that's nice," said Grandma Emily. "All I ever collected was tea cups."

"I thought you collected kids, too," said Sebastian. "Daddy said you had eight of them. Now THAT'S a collection."

Grandma Emily threw back her head and laughed. "And your daddy was the last one of them I collected."

"Grandma Emily," said Sebastian, putting his hand on her arm. "May I look at your bank?"

"Of course you may," said Grandma Emily.

She pulled up a solid wood chair for Sebastian to stand on. Sebastian hopped up. He stared into the bank. It was almost full of pennies.

"How many pennies does your bank hold?" asked Sebastian.

"About six hundred," said Grandma Emily.

"Wow!" said Sebastian. He got down from the chair. In his sweetest voice he said, "Grandma Emily. When you empty your bank next time, may I have it for my collection?" He was sure his grandmother would say yes.

But Grandma Emily said, "No, Sebastian. That old bank means a lot to me. And to Mr. Grandpa. Many a time the few pennies we saved in that bank helped us out. No. I don't want to give it away."

Chapter Four
Up in the Attic

Sebastian couldn't believe it. Grandma Emily was not going to give him her bank. It was a funny feeling not to get his way. Sebastian didn't like it a bit.

"Well," said Grandma Emily. "What shall we do? Would you like to help me bake some cookies?"

"No," said Sebastian in a rude way.

"No, thank you, Grandma Emily," said Grandma Emily.

"No, thank you, Grandmother Emily," said Sebastian. He sounded very grumpy.

"Well, how about helping me sort out the attic?" said Grandma Emily. "I started last week, but I got very tired. I need a good helper."

"All right," said Sebastian. He had never been up in Grandma Emily's attic.

"Now, this could be interesting," thought Sebastian. He followed Grandma Emily up the narrow staircase to the attic.

Sebastian stood at the top of the stairs and looked around. The attic was full of strange and wonderful things. "Wow!" said Sebastian. "This is great!"

"I'm filling a carton with your Aunt Katie's old treasures," said Grandma Emily. "Would you like to look at them?"

"Not really," said Sebastian "I would like to look at my dad's old 'stuff'."

"Your dad took his things long ago," said Grandma Emily. "But I still have boxes of things that were your Uncle Peter's."

Sebastian looked up. "Uncle Peter was a soldier. Right?"

"Yes," said Grandma Emily softly.

"And he died, didn't he?" asked Sebastian.

"Yes, Sebastian, said Grandma Emily. "He was killed in Korea. He was the first of my 'collection'".

"May I look at Uncle Peter's things?" asked Sebastian.

"I guess so, dear," said Grandma Emily. She pushed a suitcase to one side. She rolled a sleeping bag away. Then she pointed to a long wooden crate.

"Your Uncle Peter's things are in there."

Sebastian opened the wooden crate.

Sebastian took out a lot of books and notebooks.

Under the books and notebooks he found a stack of boxes.

In the first box Sebastian found a funny brown cap. Under the cap were some coloured ribbons with big coins on them.

"What are these?" asked Sebastian.

Grandma Emily looked up and said,"Those are your Uncle Peter's army medals, and that's his army cap."

Sebastian took out another box. The box was full of pencils and pocket knives and some tubes Sebastian had never seen before.

"What are these things?" asked Sebastian.

"Those are fountain pens," said Grandma Emily. "Everyone used them before there were ballpoint pens. You had to fill them with ink."

"What is ink?" asked Sebastian.

"Ink is like thin paint," said Grandma Emily. "It is dark blue or black."

"Oh," said Sebastian.

Sebastian put the box of pencils and pocket knives and fountain pens away.

There was only one box left. It was deep and square. It was too heavy for Sebastian to lift out.

"Grandma Emily," said Sebastian. "Will you help me lift out this big box?"

"Just let me straighten my old bones," said Grandma Emily. She stood up very slowly.

Chapter Five
Uncle Peter's Army

Sebastian lifted one side of the deep, square box. Grandma Emily lifted the other side of the deep, square box.

The box was almost out of the wooden crate. Sebastian could not hold onto it. Sebastian let his side drop.

"Never mind, Sebastian," said Grandma Emily. "We will try again."

This time they got the deep, square box out and put it on the floor.

Sebastian took off the lid of the deep, square box and looked inside.

"Wow!" said Sebastian. "Look at all the little men! There must be a million of them! What are they?"

"They're lead soldiers," said Grandma Emily smiling. "Mr. Grandpa and I gave Peter his first one when he was just your age. We bought it with pennies from our big glass piggy bank." Grandma Emily picked up one of the soldiers. He was wearing a red 'pill-box' hat. He had a red and blue cloak over his shoulders.

"That is the one," said Grandma Emily. "And look! Here is a British Grenadier. Here is a Russian

Cossack. Here is a Hungarian Hussar!"

"They are way cool," said Sebastian.

"Your dad loved those soldiers even more than your Uncle Peter did. When Peter was away at the war, your dad played with them all the time. He would pretend to take them all around the world."

"Really?" said Sebastian. "It is hard for me to imagine Dad being a little boy. It is hard for me to imagine Dad playing with these soldiers."

"Oh, he played with them all right," said Grandma Emily. "They were his very favourite playthings. Your dad had the most wonderful imagination of all my collection."

"The only soldiers I've ever played with are G.I. Joe's. But they're not a bit as good as these are."

Grandma Emily looked carefully at Sebastian. "Would you like these soldiers, Sebastian?" she asked.

"Oh! Yes! Grandma Emily," said Sebastian.

"If I give them to you, you must promise not to handle them too much."

"Why not?" asked Sebastian.

"Well," said Grandma Emily. "They are made of lead. And it has been found that lead is too dangerous for children to play with. That's why soldiers like these aren't to be found any more."

"What if I put them up on shelves?" said Sebastian.

"That should be just fine," said Grandma Emily. Grandma Emily noticed that Sebastian was smiling a rather mysterious smile.

"What are you up to, Sebastian?" asked Grandma Emily.

Sebastian sang this song,

I have a very secret plan
Nobody knows but me,
And when I work the whole thing out,
How glad someone will be.

Chapter Six
"What's an 'As Is'?"

Sebastian walked out to his mother's car. He was carrying two big bags. The bags were very heavy.

"Mom," said Sebastian as he got in the car. "Will you take me shopping?"

"I thought you hated shopping," said Margaret.

"I hate YOUR kind of shopping," said Sebastian. "I want to go to the big store where they sell boards."

"We go right by a place that sells boards," said Sebastian's mother. "What do you need boards for?"

"I want to build some shelves," said Sebastian. "I want to spend my own money that is in my pirate bank. I have three dollars and two cents."

"I'll bet you want the shelves for your bank collection," said Margaret.

"No," said Sebastian. "You are wrong. I want to build shelves for what is in these big bags."

"What IS in those big bags?" asked his mother.

"Some special things Grandma Emily gave me," said Sebastian. "I will show them to you when I have built my shelves."

"Building shelves is very hard to do," said the man at the store that sold boards. "Why don't you buy some shelves that are already made?"

"I do not have very much money," said Sebastian. "Shelves that are already made cost too much. I just have three dollars and two cents."

"Let's have a look at some shelves in the AS IS department," said the salesman.

"What is an AS IS department?" asked Sebastian.

"It is a department that sells things that have something wrong with them," said the salesman. "Sometimes they have a bad scratch. Sometimes they have something missing. They always cost less than things that are perfect."

Sebastian and Margaret and Sebastian's mother and the salesman all headed for the AS IS department.

They saw tables that were missing a leg. They saw chairs that had holes in their padded seats. They saw bookcases that had big scratches on their tops. They did not see any AS IS shelves.

"I'm sorry," said the salesman. "There are no AS IS shelves."

"Well, thank you anyway," said Sebastian sadly. "You really tried to help."

18

Chapter Seven
"How Much Money have You, Sebastian?"

"Where else could I look for shelves?" asked Sebastian.

"We always find neat things at garage sales," said Margaret.

"That is a very good idea," said Sebastian's mother. "We'll go home and I will look in the Edmonton Journal for some garage sales near us."

"And I will get my three dollars and two cents," said Sebastian.

Sebastian's mother made a list. "There are three garage sales near," she said. "One is just around the corner."

Sebastian and Margaret had a great time at the garage sale just around the corner. There were no shelves for sale but they found other things they wanted. Sebastian's mother bought Sebastian a very large red ball. She bought Margaret three Barbie outfits. Then they drove to the next garage sale.

It was not a very good garage sale. There were no sets of shelves. There were no things that Sebastian and Margaret wanted.

The third garage sale was quite far away. There were lots of tables and chairs and cupboards for sale. Sebastian and Margaret and Sebastian's mother looked everywhere for a small set of shelves. They could not see any.

As they were going back to the car a man came to talk to them. "Didn't you find anything you wanted?" he said.

"No," said Sebastian. "I was looking for a small set of shelves but I do not see any."

"Humm," said the man. "Wait here." The man went back into the house. He seemed to be taking a very long time.

"I think we had better go," said Sebastian's mother. Just then the man came out of the house. He was carrying a set of small shelves. The shelves were painted pink.

"My mother used these shelves for her thimble collection," said the man. "She had three hundred thimbles. She has given away all but four of her thimbles. She is happy to sell her pink thimble shelves. She wants to know the name of the boy who is buying them."

"My name is Sebastian," said Sebastian. "But I think those pink shelves may cost too much." He took his three dollars and two cents from his pocket.

"How much money do you have, Sebastian?" asked the man.

"I have three dollars and two cents," said Sebastian.

"Well, well," said the man. "That is exactly the price of these pink thimble shelves."

The man took Sebastian's three dollars and two cents. He handed Sebastian the set of small, pink thimble shelves.

"Thank you very much,' said Sebastian.

"You are very welcome, Sebastian," said the man.

Chapter Eight
Sebastian Knows How

"I can't put up pink shelves," said Sebastian. "Do we have any blue paint, Mother?"

"Yes," said his mother. "But why do you want blue paint? Your room is green."

"The shelves have to be blue," said Sebastian very firmly. "Will you find me the blue paint and a paint brush? I will paint the shelves in the garage. I learned to paint at school. Our class took turns painting the storage cupboard."

"I will find you the blue paint and a paint brush," said Sebastian's mother. "But first, you must put on some very old clothes to do your painting in."

"I have opened a new can of blue paint for you, Sebastian," said his mother. "It is paint that dries very quickly. And here is a nice new paint brush. Margaret has put newspapers on the floor in case the paint drips."

"Thank you, Mother and Margaret," said Sebastian. "You do not need to stay here. I know how to paint this set of shelves."

Sebastian's mother and Margaret went into the house.

Sebastian looked at the open can of new blue paint.

Sebastian looked at the nice new paint brush.

Sebastian looked at the small set of pink shelves leaning against the wall.

He tried to remember what his teacher had told the class about painting.

He dipped the brush deep into the can of blue paint. Sebastian pulled out the brush. Blue paint dripped everywhere. Blue paint dripped on the newspaper. Blue paint dripped on Sebastian's old shoes. Blue paint dripped on Sebastian's old slacks.

Sebastian tried to paint the back of the shelves. He had too much paint on his brush. Blue paint ran everywhere.

"What a mess!" said Sebastian. "Painting is very hard to do."

And Sebastian yelled as loud as he could…

Chapter Nine
"HELP!"

"HELP! SOMEBODY HELP ME!"

Sebastian's mother and Margaret ran into the garage.

"What a mess!" said Margaret.

"I'll get some gloves on," said Sebastian's mother. She took the brush from Sebastian's hand.

"Don't worry, Sebastian. Painting is not an easy thing to do. You must press the full brush on the inside rim of the can." She let the extra paint drip from the brush into the can.

"It is better to have too little paint than too much," said Sebastian's mother. "This is just the right amount. You take the brush now and try again."

Sebastian took the brush very carefully. He pulled it along the back of the shelves. It made a nice, neat, blue brush stroke.

"That looks fine," said Sebastian's mother. Sebastian dipped the brush very carefully into the can of blue paint. He let all the extra paint drip back into the can. Then he painted another brush stroke beside the first one.

"That's beginning to look very good," said Margaret.

As Sebastian painted he sang a painting song,

Dip the brush, but not too deep,
Press it on the rim,
Till these drips have all dropped off,
Then you can begin.

Chapter Ten
Sebastian Solves a Big Problem

Sebastian lay in his bed with his eyes wide open. It was Thursday night and he had a lot of thinking to do.

The blue paint had dried. The shelves were ready for the lead soldiers. But where could he put the shelves?

Could he nail them up?

No. That would be too hard.

Could he glue them up?

No. That would be too messy.

Could he put them on the top of a low book shelf?

Yes. He could put them on a low book shelf and lean them against the wall. But what if the shelves slipped down?

Sebastian thought a lot about that. Then he said to himself, "I will chew a whole pack of chewing gum. I will stick some of it in front of the shelves on each side. Then they will not slip down."

Sebastian had solved his big problem. He pulled the covers up over his shoulders and went to sleep.

Chapter Eleven
As Good as it Gets

Margaret and Sebastian were sitting on the front steps.

"What time does Uncle Johnnie get home on Fridays, Sebastian?" asked Margaret.

"Around six," said Sebastian.

Margaret looked at her watch.

"It's half past six," said Margaret.

"He should be home by now," said Sebastian. Sebastian was beginning to worry. He stood up and walked to the end of the sidewalk. He looked up and down the street. He said to himself, "Where IS Dad? Why is he late?"

Margaret came to watch the street too. They stood together for a long time looking first one way and then another.

Sebastian's mother came out and stood beside them.

"What time is it now, Margaret?" asked Sebastian.

"Seven," said Margaret and then she said, "Look!"

A big, blue station wagon was slowly turning the corner. It was very dusty,

"Here he comes!" shouted Sebastian.

The station wagon pulled slowly to the curb and stopped. Out of it climbed Sebastian's father. He looked very, very tired, but he smiled and said, "Hi, everybody." He opened the back of the station wagon. He took out his sample case and his briefcase and his suitcase and a big white plastic bag.

"I'll carry your sample case, Dad," said Sebastian. He picked up the sample case and headed for the house.

"I'll carry your briefcase, Uncle Johnnie," said Margaret. She picked up the briefcase and headed toward the house.

"I'll carry your suitcase, dear," said Sebastian's mother. She picked up the suitcase and headed for the house.

"And I'll carry this," said Sebastian's Dad, holding up the big white plastic bag.

At the front door Sebastian's dad took his sample case from Sebastian and gave him the big white plastic bag.

Sebastian opened the big white plastic bag and looked inside.

"Cool," said Sebastian as he took out a square black bank that looked like an office safe."

"Cool," Sebastian said again. "Thanks, Dad." Sebastian looked at Margaret. "NOW I have THREE banks, and that makes a collection."

When they were inside the house Sebastian said, "Dad, you have to come with me."

"Is it important, Sebastian?" said his dad. "I'm very, very tired."

"Yes," said Sebastian. "It is very, very important."

Sebastian led the way past his Nana's room.

Sebastian led the way past Jennifer's room.

Sebastian led the way past his mother and father's bedroom.

Sebastian led the way to a door at the end of the hall. He opened the door to his father's little office and stood back.

Sebastian's father looked inside. He looked at his small blue desk with the computer and printer on it. It was the same as he had left it. He looked at his tall, blue file cabinet. It was the same as he had left it. He looked at his low, blue bookcase. It was not the same as he had left it.

On top of his low, blue bookcase was a set of small, blue shelves.On the small, blue shelves were rows and rows of lead soldiers.

"It's Peter's army!" said Sebastian's father. He said it over and over again. "It's Peter's army! It's Peter's army!" He went to the shelves and started picking up the soldiers. "Here's the Hungarian

Hussar! Here's the British Grenadier! Here's the Russian Cossack! They're all here!" Sebastian saw a far-away look come into his father's eyes.

Sebastian wondered what his dad was thinking about.

"Now you and I each have a collection," said Sebastian.

"We sure do," said his dad. He didn't sound tired any longer. He sounded like a little kid. "But where did the little set of shelves come from? And how did it get to be the perfect colour for my study."

"I bought the shelves with my own money," said Sebastian proudly. "And I painted them myself."

"You're the greatest, Sebastian," said his dad," giving Sebastian a big hug.

Sebastian looked up. Two big tears were running down his father's cheeks.

"Thank you, Sebastian," said his dad. "It's the best present anyone ever gave me."

A feeling swept over Sebastian. A feeling he'd never had before. It was the greatest, warmest, most joyful feeling of pure happiness.

"You're welcome," said Sebastian.

Gwen Molnar is a prize winning poet and a prolific
writer of children's stories and poetry. Her children's
poetry has been dramatized on radio, television and
film. She has also painted professionally for more
than thirty years. This is her third Hodgepog Book.

Mia Hansen was born in 1970 in the town of Ayr, Ontario where she pursued illustration, cartooning, and doll making. At the age of 19 she wrote and illustrated the picture book Binky Bemelman and the Big City Begonia. From there, Mia went on to study Fine Arts at the University of Guelph.
She now resides in Vancouver, British Columbia. Along with illustration, her work includes graphic design, painting, silk-screened clothing, and handpainted wall dolls.

If you liked this book...
you might enjoy these other Hodgepog Books:

For grades 5–7

Written on the Wind
by Anne Dublin, illustrated by Avril Woodend
ISBN 1-9686899-5-7   Price $6.95

and for readers in grades 3–5,
or read them to younger kids

Ben and the Carrot Predicament
by Mar'ce Merrell, illustrated by Barbara Hartmann
ISBN 1-895836-54-9   Price $4.95

Getting Rid of Mr. Ributus
by Alison Lohans, illustrated by Barbara Hartmann
ISBN 1-895836-53-0   Price $6.95

A Real Farm Girl
By Susan Ioannou, illustrated by James Rozak
ISBN 1-895836-52-2   Price $6.95

A Gift for Johnny Know-It-All
by Mary Woodbury, illustrated by Barbara Hartmann
ISBN 1-895836-27-1   Price $5.95

Mill Creek Kids
by Colleen Heffernan, illustrated by Sonja Zacharias
ISBN 1-895836-40-9   Price $5.95

Arly & Spike
by Luanne Armstrong, illustrated by Chao Yu
ISBN 1-895836-37-9   Price $4.95

A Friend for Mr. Granville
by Gillian Richardson, illustrated by Claudette Maclean
ISBN 1-895836-38-7   Price $5.95

Maggie & Shine
by Luanne Armstrong, illustrated by Dorothy Woodend
ISBN 1-895836-67-0   Price $6.95

Butterfly Gardens
by Judith Benson, illustrated by Lori McGregor McCrae
ISBN 1-895836-71-9   Price $5.95

The Duet
by Brenda Silsbe, illustrated by Galan Akin
ISBN 0-9686899-1-4 $5.95

Jeremy's Christmas Wish
by Glen Huser, illustrated by Martin Rose
ISBN 0-9686899-2-2 $5.95

Let's Wrestle
by Lyle Weis, illustrated by Will Milner and Nat Morris
ISBN 0-9686899-4-9 $5.95

A Pocketful of Rocks
by Deb Loughead
ISBN 0-9686899-7-3 $5.95

Logan's Lake
by Margriet Ruurs, illustrated by Robin LeDrew
ISBN 1-9686899-8-1   Price $5.95

and for readers in grade 1-2,
or to read to pre-schoolers

Sebastian's Promise
by Gwen Molnar, illustrated by Kendra McCleskey
ISBN 1-895836-65-4   Price $4.95

Summer With Sebastian
by Gwen Molnar, illustrated by Kendra McClesky
ISBN 1-895836-39-5   Price $4.95

The Noise in Grandma's Attic
by Judith Benson, illustrated by Shane Hill
ISBN 1-895836-55-7   Price $4.95

Pet Fair
by Deb Loughead, illustrated by Lisa Birke
ISBN 0-9686899-3-0 $5.95